WOMBAT SMITH

Wombat Takes on Tasmania

written by
ANNE SAUTEL

rated by
STEWART

D1301945

Lobster Press ™

Wombat Smith: Wombat Takes on Tasmania
Text © 2006 by Anne Sautel
Illustrations © 2006 by Scott Stewart

JPF
Sautel

Published by Lobster Press"
1620 Sherbrooke Street West, Suites C & D
Montréal, Québec   H3H 1C9
Tel. (514) 904-1100 • Fax (514) 904-1101 • www.lobsterpress.com

Publisher: Alison Fripp
Editors: Alison Fripp, Karen Li & Meghan Nolan
Editorial Assistants: Penny Smart & Morgan Dambergs
Graphic Design & Production: Tammy Desnoyers

We acknowledge the financial support of the Government of Canada
through the Book Publishing Industry Development Program (BPIDP)
for our publishing activities.

The Canada Council | Le Conseil des Arts
for the Arts | du Canada

We acknowledge the support of
the Canada Council for the Arts
for our publishing program.

Library and Archives Canada Cataloguing in Publication

Sautel, Anne, 1934-
      Wombat takes on Tasmania / Anne Sautel ; Scott Stewart, illustrator.

(Wombat Smith)
ISBN-13: 978-1-897073-32-2
ISBN-10: 1-897073-32-1

      1. Marsupials--Juvenile fiction. I. Stewart, Scott II. Title.
III. Series: Sautel, Anne, 1934- Wombat Smith.

PS8637.A82W64 2006   jC813'.6   C2005-905007-1

Printed and bound in Canada.

To the memory of Fraser,
And to Rob,
Sara and Andrew.

– Anne Sautel

Chapter 1

When Wombat became a member of the Smith family, no one, except perhaps the occasional stranger meeting him for the first time, seemed to notice that he appeared a little different. The biggest difference, everyone agreed, was probably his hair, for although it was brown like Mr. and Mrs. Smith's, and his sister Mary's too, it grew not only on his head, but all over his body.

Mary, who had been almost five years old when Wombat first arrived, helped to look after him while he was still a baby, feeding him special milk from a bottle and bathing him in sweet-scented water filled with bubbles. But Wombat matured faster than Mary, just like Sandalfoot the dog, whose years were each counted as seven instead of only one. And while Mary wished she could be like Wombat and grow up quickly too, Wombat would rather have been like her so that he could go to school. For when it came time to enroll them in the first grade, Mrs. Smith, counting Wombat's age in sevens as she always did, had to say he was fourteen.

"I am sorry, but I can't have Wombat in my class," Mary's teacher had explained to Mrs. Smith. "The other children would be distracted by an older student in the room."

So Wombat did not go to school to study, but Mary was glad to teach him everything she learned. Every evening, after he had wiped the ice cream and chocolate cake from the fur around his mouth, Mary would open her schoolbooks on the kitchen table and teach him how to read and how to sound out words. It wasn't long before Wombat had finished reading all of Mary's books.

Mr. Smith encouraged him too, giving him books that weren't very difficult to read. Wombat spent his days learning all he could about the trees and the plants that grew in all the countries of the world. He read about the insects and the reptiles, but most of all, he enjoyed reading about the animals.

One day, Wombat found a book with the word "Australia" in large, black type on the cover. Beneath, in smaller letters, he read the word "marsupials." After sounding it out very carefully, for he had never seen the word "marsupials" before, he opened the book and began to read.

"Marsupial mothers carry their babies in a pouch," he exclaimed. Then he ran to the living room, where a photograph, taken when he was just a baby, sat on the table in the corner.

The picture showed mostly his eyes and ears above the opening of the leather pouch that hung on long straps from Mrs. Smith's shoulders.

He ran outside to the garden, where Mrs. Smith was pulling the weeds from around her flowers. "Did you know?" he asked, pausing to take a deep breath in his excitement. "Did you know you are a marsupial?"

"No, dear, *I'm* not," she replied gently. "*You* are." She put her hand on Wombat's shoulder. "We found you all alone, without a family, when we were in Tasmania. And as soon as we saw you, we knew you would be a perfect addition to our family." Mrs. Smith put both her arms around Wombat and held him very close. "Is there anything more you would like to know?"

"Where is Tasmania? Is it far away?" Wombat asked.

"It's a small island off the mainland of Australia," she answered. "Very far away. All the way across the ocean."

"Well, if I'm a marsupial, then I suppose I should know more about them," Wombat decided, crawling out of Mrs. Smith's arms.

Wombat looked through all the books in

the house without finding one picture of a marsupial, so he decided to go to the library. "Can we go there now?" he asked excitedly, after telling Mrs. Smith what he wanted to do.

Mrs. Smith agreed that it was a good idea. "But I can't go with you today. I will take you there tomorrow," she said.

"Please let me go today. I can take the bus," Wombat insisted, for he could not wait any longer to find out what marsupials were like.

Mrs. Smith was a little anxious to let him go on the bus alone, for the library was several blocks away. However, she gave him the money he would need, and a cookie for him to eat, before she put him on the bus.

As the bus went down the street, Wombat looked at the buildings that they passed, especially the bakery that sold his favorite cookies, and the small convenience store where he sometimes got a chocolate bar. He had no trouble remembering the stop where he was to get off, for he had gone on the bus with Mrs. Smith several times before.

At the library, Wombat climbed the steps to a door with a large window. Standing on his toes to peer through the glass, he could see the room inside. The door was very heavy, and although he pulled as hard as he could, he was not able to open it. A father arriving with his young son and daughter opened the door and let Wombat in. After thanking him, Wombat went inside and walked up to a lady with gray hair who sat at a long desk.

She stood up and leaned across the desk when Wombat greeted her. "You'll need to stand on a chair so that I can see you better," she said, looking down at him.

"Did you know I am a marsupial?" Wombat asked as he moved a chair closer to the desk.

The librarian looked a little surprised. "That's funny," she said. "I always thought you were a Smith." She waited as Wombat climbed onto the wooden seat. "That's much better. Now, what are you looking for today?"

"I am looking for marsupials," he replied. He leaned over to watch as she typed the word "Australia" into the computer that sat between them on the desk.

"Wait right where you are," she said, standing up. "Don't move, and don't fall off the chair." Then she disappeared down one of the long rows of shelves filled with tightly-packed books.

It seemed like a very long time before she returned, and Wombat, who had been standing very still, just as he had been told, began to worry that he might lose his balance. He reached out to steady himself on the desk. To his relief, the librarian did not seem to notice that he had moved when she returned, probably because she was distracted by the heavy book she was carrying.

When she placed the book on the desk, Wombat flipped open the cover and turned a few pages. Although the book was very thick, the printed words were small, and the only picture he could find was of a tree with yellow flowers.

"Wattle tree," he read out loud, which seemed to please the librarian very much. "It's a very pretty tree," he added quickly, "but it's not a marsupial."

The librarian watched as he turned the other pages without reading any words. "How old are you?" she asked finally.

Wombat thought for a moment. The question was not an easy one to answer, because Mary's age was counted in ones, and Sandalfoot's age in sevens.

"I think I'm two in people years," he answered thoughtfully. "But in dog years, I'd be fourteen."

"I see," she said kindly, even though she did not really seem to see at all.

"Thank you for the book," he said, "but I'd like to look at one with pictures, please."

"You don't look fourteen, so perhaps a book with more pictures would be better." And after going to another side of the room, she came back with three thin books that seemed much easier to carry. "I think these are what you want," she said, as she put them on the desk in front of Wombat. Then, because the librarian said she had other work to do, he took the books to a quiet table, where he was glad to look through them alone.

He opened the first book and looked at the pictures of the birds. There were brightly-colored lorikeets and a lyrebird with its long, curved tail. In the second book were reptiles, and he saw a frilled-neck lizard and a black tiger snake. *This is very interesting*, thought Wombat, *but not what I came to see.*

Inside the cover of the third book, however, Wombat found what he was looking for. In bold letters was the word "Marsupials." He hurried through the pictures of the kangaroo, the wallaby, and the pademelon. At last, he turned a page, and a fur-covered face with a large, flat nose and round eyes—a face that could have been his own—looked back at him. Underneath the picture were the words "Wombat, Native of Australia."

"I'm not the only one!" he cried excitedly,

for he had never seen anyone who looked like him anywhere in his city. The white-haired man reading a book nearby looked up with a frown. Then Wombat, remembering that he was in a library, spoke in a very quiet voice. "I'm not so different, after all," he explained, showing the man the picture. The man admitted there seemed to be a slight resemblance, and Wombat wished his family could see the picture too. He would have made a copy of the picture for them, if he had known how to draw, and he decided right then that he would learn to draw, just as soon as he had the time. In his hurry to take the good news to his family, Wombat ran all the way home without waiting for the bus.

Mrs. Smith was standing at the door, and she greeted him with a tight hug, for he had been gone a long time. "You must be hungry," she said, handing him a cookie filled with chocolate chips.

"Did you know," he began, pausing for a moment to swallow the cookie crumbs, "that there are others who look just like me?"

"Yes, dear," she replied, surprised that no one had thought to mention it. "There are many others much like you."

At first, Wombat found this news very exciting, but then he began to question things he had never thought about before. Was this really where he belonged, he wondered sadly? Suddenly, for the first time, he did not feel as if he were really a member of the Smith family.

Chapter 2

During the next few days, Wombat could think of nothing but the picture in the book, and when he slept, wombats filled his dreams. A strange new feeling stretched down into his stomach and became an ache stronger than the one he had felt the day he gobbled too many chocolate cookies. He lost his appetite and found there was nothing he wanted to eat, not even the chocolate layer cake from the little bakery down the street. His fur became dull and matted, and no matter how hard Mary scrubbed, she could not get it smooth again.

"I know something is troubling you, dear," Mrs. Smith said one night as she tucked him in his bed. "Can I do anything to help?" she asked.

When Wombat did not answer, she said, "You don't have to tell me if you don't want to, but I think I understand. I think you need to go to Australia. Not to the mainland, but to the island, Tasmania, where we found you. When you meet others like you, perhaps you will learn more about yourself." With that, Mrs. Smith gave Wombat a kiss on his nose and left the room.

After Mrs. Smith had gone, Wombat snuggled comfortably under the covers. He hadn't told her anything, and yet she understood. He fell into a deep sleep that night, thinking happily about the exciting trip he was going to take and all the wombats he was going to meet.

✳✳✳

"Maybe you will like it better there," Mary said sadly, when she heard that he was leaving. "Maybe you won't come back."

"If Wombat decides to stay away, I'm sure he will come back to visit us," Mr. Smith said.

"And I will write to you," Wombat added, and Mary smiled, for no one had ever written to her before.

Mr. and Mrs. Smith were reluctant to let him go alone, but Wombat knew he would be all right, for he had gone all the way to the library by himself on the bus. Finally, they agreed to let him go if all the arrangements were made ahead of time, so that he would be looked after along the way. And Mrs. Smith was able to arrange a tour into the bush for him, with a guide who she and Mr. Smith had met when they were in Tasmania.

When it was time to go, Mrs. Smith helped Wombat pack his big knapsack with the things that he would need: his toothbrush, his brush and comb, a washcloth for his ears, and a pen and some notepaper so he would not forget to write to them. There was a small tent to take for protection when he was in the bush, and maps to read in case he got lost. After Sandalfoot had licked Wombat's face one last time, Wombat got into the car and sat beside Mary in the back seat.

"Good-bye Sandalfoot," he called out, and the dog gave his tail a very little wag, for he did not seem to understand why Wombat was going away.

When the Smiths arrived at the airport, Wombat began to feel nervous about traveling alone, for the building was very large, and filled with many busy people. Mr. and Mrs. Smith took him to the counter to pick up the tickets that would get him to the city of Melbourne in Australia, and then to Tasmania.

"We can't go with you through this gate," Mr. Smith said. "So this is where we have to say good-bye."

Mary wiped tears from her eyes. Then she took something small and square from her pocket. It was loosely wrapped in white tissue paper, and smelled very much like apple blossoms. "I've used it once," she said, handing it to him. "It will get you clean, but it won't make any bubbles."

"Maybe you will send pictures once in a while," Mr. Smith said gruffly, trying to hide his sadness as he pulled a small camera from his jacket pocket. Then he handed Wombat the money he would need for the trip and extra to pay for the airplane tickets if he wanted to come home.

"Be careful," Mrs. Smith said, kissing

Wombat lightly on his large, flat nose. She handed him a green gift bag covered with painted silver bells that she had saved from Christmas. "Watch out for cars on the road, and Tasmanian devils in the bush, and farmers with—" she paused to watch him take a woolen sweater from the bag. It was red, his favorite color, and decorated with diamond shapes of blue and green around the neck. "To keep you warm in the bush," she explained.

"Thank you," Wombat said, and because he was upset, he did not think to ask her about the other dangers in Tasmania. He could only think about the sadness he was feeling, now that it was time to leave. After kissing Mr. Smith and Mary, he put his arms around Mrs. Smith, and suddenly, he could not let her go, remembering that it might be a long time before he saw her, or any of them, again. And yet, if he stayed, he would always wonder about the wombats, and about himself. Letting go of Mrs. Smith, he turned and walked quickly away, before he could change his mind.

Chapter 3

"Are you old enough to be traveling alone?" an attendant asked Wombat as he entered the plane.

"Yes," he answered bravely, trying to hide his nervousness. "I am fourteen." Then he added thoughtfully, "I think that would be my age in wombat years." Because the attendant looked surprised, he thought he should explain. "They will probably count my age in Sandalfoot's years." She was very slow at understanding, and so he added, "Of course, that's only if wombats count their years in sevens."

"Sevens?" she asked, still confused. "Well, the seats are all numbered," she said quickly, before he had a chance to say anything more, "but would you like help?"

"No, thank you," he replied. "I've learned to read numbers."

As Wombat walked down the long aisle of the plane, he saw that the seat numbers were written high above the seats, so he had to balance on his toes to read them. It was much easier to read the numbers while looking down at them in a school book on the kitchen table, he remembered, and he wondered why no one had thought to put the numbers on the floor.

When he found his seat, he saw that it was by the window, and he had to slip past the two people who were already sitting in his row. The man sitting next to the aisle stood up so Wombat wouldn't step on his feet.

After squeezing by the lady in the middle, Wombat sat down and tucked his knapsack under the seat in front of him, before putting on his safety belt. As the plane began to taxi down the runway, Wombat sat very still and watched the buildings outside his window. They began to slide past very quickly, and then the plane lifted into the air. As Wombat watched the ground move farther away, he felt a funny sensation in his stomach, and he wondered if birds felt this way when they were learning to fly. He would have asked the lady sitting next to him, but she had her eyes closed, so he turned back to face the window.

When the plane was high in the air, the lady opened her eyes and turned to him. "Will this be the first time you will see Australia?" she asked.

"I have seen it before," Wombat answered. "But only in a book."

"One can always tell a tourist by the camera," she explained. Then she opened a paper bag and held it out to him. "Would you like a cookie?" she asked.

"Yes, thank you," Wombat replied, adding hopefully, as he peered inside the bag, "I do like chocolate chips."

"There aren't any chocolate chips in these cookies," she apologized. "Only wattle seeds. I baked them myself."

"They are very good," Wombat said politely

as he took a bite into his cookie, even though it had a very unusual flavor. "In fact," he added, after taking a couple more bites, "if I knew how to cook, I would ask you for the recipe."

The lady smiled and handed him another. "There are lots of pictures to take in Melbourne, if you are staying for a while," she said.

"Not very long," Wombat replied. "I'm going to Tasmania to look for wombats in the bush."

"Are you taking pictures for a magazine?" the lady asked with interest, and she showed Wombat the nature magazine that she was reading. She seemed disappointed when Wombat shook his head. "Well, they are nice creatures to look at anyway," she said. "One of my favorites at the zoo."

"Oh, I'd rather not see them in a cage," Wombat said, feeling very uncomfortable at the thought. "That's why I'm going into the bush."

Then, because all the cookies were gone, the woman put away the bag and opened another magazine to read. Wombat turned back to the window to watch the ocean below. He must have slept for a little while, for when he woke, the ocean seemed to be rising toward them. Suddenly, he spotted a large expanse of land covered with tiny buildings. He watched excitedly as the buildings grew larger, and by the time he felt the wheels of the plane touch the ground, the buildings had grown to their actual size.

***

The sun was shining when Wombat stepped out of the plane in Melbourne. He followed the lady who had sat next to him into the airport, and she went with him into a shop that sold magazines and candy. He was glad that she could help him pick out the right amount of money he needed to buy postage stamps for the postcards he planned to send, for Australian money did not look like the money he was used to.

"Would it be all right if I took your picture?" he asked the lady shyly, before she could walk away.

Because she seemed so pleased that he had asked her, he took more than one. He would have asked to take a picture of her cookies too, if they hadn't all been eaten, for it would have been a nice picture to hang on his bedroom wall.

Because the plane to Tasmania would not leave until the next morning, Wombat had planned to spend one day touring the city of Melbourne. Now that he was there, he bought a hat with a wide brim to keep the sun out of his eyes, and he was pleased to find that he looked like the other tourists who were taking pictures of the city.

He went into the aquarium building, and after looking at the sharks, he took a boat ride on the Yarra River. He couldn't see any sharks there, so he took pictures of the casino, the small shops, and the restaurants along the riverbank. Then he walked through the big marketplace and took pictures of the stalls with the different foods that were for sale. He bought a large bag of wattle seeds and some other food to take into the bush. He enjoyed himself immensely, but by the end of the day, his feet were sore, and he was very tired and hungry. He went to the first restaurant he found and limped inside.

No sooner had he sat down, when a girl wearing a crisp white shirt, with a name tag too small to read, stood over him with a pad and pencil in her hand.

"I'll just have a salad," he said, without looking at the menu. "A large one," he added, for he was very hungry.

"What kind of dressing?" she asked.

Wombat thought for a moment. "Chocolate," he whispered guiltily, for he would not have been allowed to have that at home.

"We don't have chocolate," she said. "We

have garlic or plain oil and vinegar."

"Then I will have the garlic, please," he said, for he didn't want anything to be plain on this special trip. "And for dessert," he added quickly, before she had time to walk away, "I'll have chocolate cake and ice cream with my chocolate cookie."

After Wombat had finished eating, his full stomach made him very sleepy. He got into a taxi, and handed the driver the piece of paper his mother had given him with the name and address of the hotel where he would be staying. They traveled quickly down several streets, before the taxi stopped at a building with the name and the address on a sign. Wombat gave the driver the money that he owed for the ride before leaving the cab, and then he entered the hotel. After signing his name at the desk, he took the elevator to the third floor hallway, and opened the door to his room.

Wombat set his camera down on the small table by the bed and hung his sweater very carefully in the closet. After filling the tub with warm water, he scrubbed himself with the soap Mary had given him, until the smell of apple blossoms filled the room. Then he dried his fur with the warm air of the hair dryer left beside the sink for the convenience of the guests. When he had washed the chocolate from the fur around his mouth, he brushed his teeth twice and then crawled into bed.

After he had closed his eyes, he thought about the next day, and wondered if he would find wombats as soon as he was in the bush. Growing more excited, he had to count wattle seed cookies in his mind to put himself to sleep.

Chapter 4

The next morning, the man at the hotel desk phoned for a taxi to take Wombat to the airport. Wombat was very glad that he did not have long to wait until it was time to board the plane to the island, and soon he was in the air, crossing the stretch of water called Bass Strait. When the plane landed at the airport in Tasmania, the bus that would take Wombat to the outpost was waiting for him. They traveled for what seemed a long time, and Wombat became impatient, as he was very anxious to meet other wombats.

When they finally reached the outpost, he discovered that it was located in a clearing at the edge of the woods. He thought that Mr. and Mrs. Smith must have made a mistake in arranging for a tour, because he did not need a guide when the bush was right there in front of him. Not wanting to take the time just then to go into the outpost, and thinking he could come back later, he set out immediately into the bush. He wandered deep into the wilderness, and as he looked for wombats, he thought about the food he had bought at the market. No matter how hard he tried, he could not make up his mind about what he was going to have for lunch.

I will try a taste of everything, he thought to himself. *And then I will be able to choose.* He ate some fruit: a bush tomato, a quandong, and an illawarra plum, and as he continued to walk, he tried all the other food in his bag. But when he was done, he still wasn't sure, and he had to taste it all again. Because it was all so good, Wombat decided to wait until lunchtime to make up his mind.

He continued to walk for the rest of the morning, and although he was certain he heard several animals in the bush, he saw only a couple of mice, and a black tiger snake that raised its head before sliding noiselessly away. The morning's lack of success disappointed him, and when he came to a stream, he sat down on its bank. His stomach was already getting a lunchtime feeling, but when he opened his bag, he saw, to his surprise, that all the food was gone, except a few wattle seeds at the bottom of the bag. "I'm going to be hungry now," he grumbled. "I tasted everything too much, and didn't save anything for my lunch." Realizing that he was not likely to come upon a restaurant in the bush, he looked around for something that would make a nice meal. He tried chewing a handful of the grass. It was safe to eat, but not very appetizing without some salad dressing. Then he tested the leaves from the eucalyptus tree beside him and found that they didn't taste any better.

He remembered the wattle seeds in his bag, and, using his lap as a plate, he mixed a handful of grass with some shredded eucalyptus leaves, and sprinkled the wattle seeds on top. The seeds weren't sweet like the cookies had been, but he enjoyed them once he became used to their flavor. *This would be a very nice salad in a restaurant,* thought Wombat. *I must remember it in case I should write a recipe book.* He finished his meal quickly, and because he was still hungry, he carefully picked the remaining wattle seeds off his lap and popped them into his mouth. *The salad was good, but not as good as the cookies on the plane,* he decided, as he lay down beside the stream and closed his eyes. *And those cookies were not as good as the cookie I had before I rode on the bus to the library.* He thought carefully for a moment. *And that one wasn't as good as the one I ate after I got off.*

He thought about the chocolate cake he had eaten on his first birthday, and before he could think about the one on his second birthday, he was interrupted by a splash beside him. He sat up in time to see a strange creature with a duck's bill and a beaver's tail swimming in the stream nearby. *A platypus*, he thought,

reaching into his knapsack for his camera. The startled animal opened its mouth with a growl, and several shrimp floated from its cheek. Then it dived into the water, leaving only a series of ripples as Wombat took its picture.

"An expensive lunch in a restaurant," Wombat said, looking at the shrimp floating on the surface of the water, "but not one that appeals to me." To take away his hunger, he knelt to lap up the fresh water of the stream. After a while, he had to stop, for his tongue and jaw began to ache. "It would be much easier if I'd brought my blue mug from home," he sighed.

After leaving the stream, Wombat walked farther into the bush, looking behind every tree for wombats. He saw very few animals during the day, but as the sun began to set, many different sounds filled the woods around him. The snapping of dry twigs among the bushes told him of the creatures, too small for him to see, that were keeping their distance, afraid to get close to him. He stood very still, hoping that in the silence a wombat might appear.

At one point, he heard footsteps coming closer to him, and peering into the shadows of the bushes, he could see the outline of a small animal staring back at him. It took a few steps closer, stopping where the moonlight shone on its pointed nose and highlighted the white stripes of its fur. *This is certainly no relative of mine*, Wombat thought, for it looked more like a rat that he had once seen while walking Sandalfoot in the field near his house.

The animal also reminded him of a picture he had seen in the book at the library. Wombat wished that he had made a copy of the picture in a notebook, if he had a notebook, for he would be able to look at the drawing now. And he made up his mind right then that he would get a notebook, just as soon as he had the time.

"I'm Wombat Smith," he said, introducing himself politely. Then, to show that he was good at remembering names, he added, "And you must be a bandicoot. I saw your picture in a book."

When Wombat spoke, the animal ran away, and Wombat thought that perhaps the bandicoot was upset to hear that its picture was in a book. *I guess it saw my camera and didn't want its picture taken again*, he thought. *I must remember, when I meet the wombats, not to tell them about the book.*

He became very tired as he continued on his way. His pace slowed in the darkness, and he stumbled over stones and fallen branches. He wondered if he would have found some wombats if he had been able to go faster. *Slow poke. Slow poke*, a boobook owl seemed to call to him as it flew away, disturbed by the intrusion.

He felt very discouraged as he set up his tent. He crawled inside and lay awake, listening to the strange, unfamiliar noises of the night. He shivered. In the darkness, he felt terribly alone.

Chapter 5

Wombat must have finally drifted into a light sleep, for he was wakened suddenly by something cold touching his hand. Then he felt a wet tongue. For a moment, he thought he was lying on the grass in the garden and that Sandalfoot was nudging him to play. But when he sat up, he saw that the tongue did not belong to a dog, but to what appeared to be a small kangaroo. "A pademelon," Wombat whispered, thinking back to the library book, for the creature was too small to be a wallaby. The pademelon backed out of the tent, and Wombat followed slowly, hoping that the animal would not be frightened away like the others.

"You must be very hungry," he said, as the pademelon began to lick the wattle seeds caught in the fur on Wombat's hand. Then, as the pademelon took another step closer, Wombat noticed that it was limping. "Your foot is bleeding," he said. He remembered the time he had cut his own foot, and Mrs. Smith had covered it with a sticky bandage. Wombat hadn't thought to bring any sticky bandages with him, so he hoped his washcloth would do instead. He was just about to take it from his knapsack when a terrible scream rose behind him.

He turned, and a short distance away, almost hidden in the trees, was the shadow of an animal. Wombat and the pademelon stood motionless with fear. For a moment, the shadow did not move. Then the creature stepped out from the trees and opened its mouth very wide. Its sharp teeth gleamed in the moonlight, and Wombat suddenly recalled a picture he had seen at the library. A picture of the creature his mother had warned him about. A Tasmanian devil!

Wombat turned to the trembling pademelon and realized that the Tasmanian devil must have been hunting the injured animal. Wombat began to pull the pademelon to help it run faster as it limped after him. For a moment, the Tasmanian devil stared at them without moving. Wombat knew, however, that once it decided to give chase, it would catch them easily.

"Faster. You have to run *faster*," Wombat

gasped, already out of breath. The pademelon had grown tired and was lagging behind. "We have to find a place to hide," panted Wombat. "Or we'll be caught soon!"

He thought he could hear the Tasmanian devil's footsteps right behind him. He thought he could feel its breath on his tail. And finally, when he thought there was no hope for escape, Wombat spotted a tunnel in the ground a short distance away. He pulled the pademelon toward the entrance and pushed the injured animal inside. Wombat tried to follow, but the hole was very narrow, not big enough for his stomach or his large rear end. At the last possible minute,

Wombat sucked in his breath to pull in his stomach, and was able to squeeze every part of himself inside – every part except his bottom.

He heard the footsteps stop behind him, and he closed his eyes, afraid to think of his poor stump of a tail and what might happen next. He took a deep breath and waited. Nothing happened. He listened carefully. There was no sound behind him. Slowly, he backed out of the hole and looked around. The Tasmanian devil had gone!

After checking himself all over, especially his tail, Wombat helped the pademelon out of the tunnel. Wombat brushed the dirt from his fur and then examined his sweater. "Oh dear," he sighed. "I hope my apple blossom soap will get this clean. I don't think I'll find any laundry soap in the bush."

Then, using the washcloth that was packed in his knapsack, Wombat dabbed the blood from the pademelon's foot and wrapped the animal's wound. "You should have a name," Wombat said, as they rested close to the entrance of the tunnel. He remembered that the baby pademelons in the library book were called

Joey, and it seemed like a very good name. Of course, the young wallabies and kangaroos were Joey too, but since the pademelon would probably never see the book, he decided not to mention it. "I will call you Joey," he whispered, and he placed his arms around the pademelon's neck, happy to have some company at last.

Chapter 6

For a long time, Wombat sat silently with the pademelon, and although he began to feel very tired, he did not allow himself to fall asleep. He remained still and stared into the darkness, watching for any sign of danger and listening to the many different sounds that began to surround them.

As his eyes became more accustomed to the darkness, he could see a hungry little bettong keeping a suspicious eye on the long-nosed potoroo also digging for roots in the rustling grass nearby. Then he saw a sugar glider spread the loose skin between its legs to sail gracefully through the air, and a ringtail possum hung down from a branch above Wombat's head to get a closer look. An anteater waddled out from behind a bush, and as it passed Wombat's feet, its long tongue darted out to pick up the ant that had crawled onto Wombat's leg. *A spiny anteater*, Wombat thought as its fur brushed against his leg. *A very spiny anteater.*

Then the sound of several animals could be heard coming toward them. As the footsteps came closer, Wombat smelled a strong odor, an

unpleasant one that he recognized with embarrassment, for he remembered smelling like that once when he had gone too long without a bath. The scent grew even stronger, and he was excited to see several wombats waddle out from between the trees. As though noticing him for the first time, the animals stopped and raised their heads to sniff the air. Wombat held his breath, not daring to make a sound, but the wild wombats must not have recognized his apple blossom scent, for they turned and bumped into each other as they ran away through the underbrush.

"Wait," he cried. "I'm a wombat—just like you!" *Well, not exactly like you,* he thought as he pictured himself in his traveling outfit. He quickly took off his hat and red sweater, and tucked them into his knapsack. "Come along, Joey," he said. "We'll look for another bunch of wombats that haven't seen my sweater yet."

✱ ✱ ✱

It was almost dawn by the time they finally found a group of wombats in a grove of eucalyptus trees. Not wanting to frighten them, Wombat put down his backpack and knelt on the ground. As he crawled slowly toward them, he thought he heard laughter coming from a branch above his head. He became embarrassed, realizing that he was in the midst of strangers without his clothes on. But looking up, he found that it was only a kookaburra's laughing call he had heard, and because the wombats did not pay any attention to his lack of clothing, he began to feel more comfortable.

"Oh, dear!" he sighed, sampling the moss that the wombats seemed to enjoy eating. "This would taste much better with a little garlic dressing." He wished, too, that he had brought a fork, for he suddenly remembered that he had not washed the mud from his hands.

With each hour that passed, Wombat became more and more tired, but he knew that he would not be able to rest until morning if he wanted to be accepted by these nighttime animals. Finally, with the coming of daylight, the creatures lumbered away, and Wombat, helping Joey, followed them to their tunnels, where they would disappear to sleep for the day.

"I've never slept in a hole in the ground," Wombat said to Joey, "and I don't think I want to try it, for you never know what you might find underground."

Wombat gathered two large piles of fallen leaves and arranged them underneath the trees. "These can be our beds," he said. Then he collected dead branches he found lying on the ground and pushed them into the earth close together to form a fence around Joey and himself while they slept. That night, as he lay on his makeshift mattress, he wished that the Tasmanian devil had not forced him to leave his tent.

"I should have learned how to build a proper shelter at Boy Scout camp," he said sadly. "If I had gone to Boy Scout camp." And he decided right then that he would become a Boy Scout, just as soon as he had the time.

✳ ✳ ✳

At first, Wombat found it exciting being in the bush, as he watched the birds and animals that he had never seen before. The various odors, too, were unfamiliar, and there were many different sounds that were new to him. But the wombats continued to ignore him, even though he picked tender leaves for them and gathered the special moss they loved to eat. After several days, they let him get closer to them, but when he tried to brush their fur and clean around their mouths, they backed away from him again.

When he had slept for a couple of weeks on the cold, hard ground without a blanket, Wombat began to cough and sneeze. He longed for his bed with the soft mattress and the downy pillows. Not only was he coming down with a head cold and a sore throat, he didn't have any more wattle seeds, and his meals of leaves and grass seemed tasteless without them. Occasionally, he would find some small red

berries, which became the only food he enjoyed.

As several more days passed, he became more miserable. The wombats, although not objecting to his presence, did not become more friendly. And although Joey stayed with Wombat, he would not play like Sandalfoot. Wombat's nose ran and his throat itched, and he was in a strange place in the company of strangers—wombats that could not speak a single word. He wished for his home, and his bed, and a bowl of hot chicken soup. He wished for cookies, cake, and salads with garlic dressing. He wished for his sister's schoolbooks, and his father's words of encouragement. He wished for his mother's arms around him. And he wished he could remember why it had become important that his family did not look like him, for suddenly it did not seem to matter at all.

He realized that, although he had been born a wombat, it was the Smiths who loved him and were his family now. "I have to leave you," he said to Joey. The pademelon leaned against Wombat to lick the berry juice from his chin. "Your leg is all better, so you can go." Then Wombat spoke very quietly. "If you want to be happy, you have to go back home to where you feel you really belong."

After putting on his sweater, Wombat took one last picture of Joey. Then he put his arms around the pademelon's neck for a hug, and Joey rolled his eyes. *Perhaps the animal is sad because he understands*, Wombat thought wishfully. *Or perhaps my arms were too tight around his neck.* "I guess I'll never know," Wombat sighed.

Although he was excited by the thought of going home, he could not leave before trying to get the attention of the wombats, in the hope that, just once, they would give him a sign that they had accepted him. "I have something important to tell you," he said, but only one wombat stopped eating to look at him. Wombat turned away sadly, but then, thinking that the wombat might be waiting for an explanation, he stopped. "I'm not really like you after all," he said. "I'm not meant to live like you, here in the bush. And that's why I have to go." As Wombat began to leave, he looked back one last time, hoping the wombats would show some sign of disappointment that he was leaving them. But they had all turned their backs on him, so he walked away.

Chapter 7

Wombat discovered, to his surprise, that he had no trouble finding his way back through the bush. *Just like Sandalfoot,* he thought as he remembered when the dog had found its way home after straying too far away. Finally, when the heaviest part of the growth of trees ended, he reached the road where the outpost stood within a short distance. As he hurried up to the door, he grew more excited. It would not be long now before he would be on the bus that would take him back to the airport, and then—then he would be on his way home. Soon he would be with his family again.

Because it was getting late, he was afraid that it might be past the outpost's dinner hour, and he hurried into the building, feeling very hungry. The room inside looked comfortable, with armchairs and a small writing desk with a variety of postcards on the top, and he paused for a moment to look at them. There was one with a picture of a wallaby, looking very much like a pademelon, which he thought would be nice to send to Mary. He took the postcard and put the right amount of money in the small dish left on the desk for that purpose.

Then he sat down and picked up the pen. "I am having a good time," he wrote, for he did not want his family to worry. "This wallaby almost looks like my friend Joey. You will see what I mean when I show you the pictures that I took." He then addressed the postcard, and after putting on one of the stamps he had bought in Melbourne, he slipped it into a mailbox that was there for the convenience of the guests.

There was the sound of china dishes nearby, and the smell of food came to him through an open doorway. Thankful that he was not too late for dinner after all, he hurried into the dining room and sat down at a small, unoccupied table. The few people who were there did not seem to want to make his acquaintance, for they turned away, as though hoping he would not speak to them.

The waitress, too, hesitated for a moment before going to him to take his order. He had a hard time deciding what to eat, for he would have liked to have a taste of everything. Finally, he chose a cup of hot chocolate and a dish of chocolate ice cream with chocolate syrup, even though he knew that a bowl of hot soup might have been better for his cold. He had to give his order several times before the waitress understood, for his sore throat made his voice sound more like squeals than words.

The lady sitting alone at the next table called the waitress to her. "That new guest looks like he's been living in the bush for a very long time," Wombat heard her whisper. "I can't see very well without my glasses, but he would look almost like a wombat if he wasn't wearing a sweater."

Since the lady was looking at him, Wombat gave her his biggest smile. He hoped that she would join him, for it had been a long time since he had been able to have a conversation. *She must be late for something*, thought Wombat, for she left the room in a hurry, without finishing her coffee.

The waitress returned, and Wombat could hardly wait until she had placed his food on the table. He lowered his head closer to the dish in front of him. Without thinking, he stuck out his tongue and was about to lick the ice cream when he noticed the waitress looking at him. Suddenly, he realized what he was doing. He

would not lick the food in a dish when he was at the table at home, or eat with his hands, as he had been doing in the bush. He had been taught to use a spoon.

However, he found eating with a spoon more awkward than he remembered. The ice cream slipped off each time he tried to take a bite, but he finally managed to eat it all. The hot chocolate, too, would have been easier to drink if he could have lapped it up with his tongue, but he forced himself to drink it from the cup. Feeling out of place, he wanted to get out of the room as quickly as possible, but he took the time to thank the waitress. Then he left money for the bill and a generous tip, before leaving the table to find a washroom.

He went back into the lobby and found the door to the bathroom. As he hurried toward the sink to wash his hands, he glimpsed something in the mirror. Something unfamiliar and dirty, with matted fur covering its head and its face. Something in a red sweater that had to be him.

"No," he squeaked hoarsely. "That's not me," he squealed, again and again, until he lost his voice entirely.

Realizing he would have to improve his appearance if he wanted to be allowed on the bus to the airport, he poured some warm water in the basin and washed his face and hands. Then he tried to wash the matted fur on his legs and feet with the liquid soap he found sitting on the counter. *I will never get clean this way*, he thought, splashing the water over himself, for he was used to having baths in a tub. And he remembered sadly the baths his mother used to give him in warm water filled with bubbles.

If I fill the sink to the brim, Wombat thought, *there might be enough water to sit in.*

Quickly, he took off his sweater, and after several attempts, he managed to scramble up onto the counter. Then he lowered himself carefully into the sink. The warm water felt very nice, but it would have been better if most of it had not overflowed onto the floor and the counter. And because his large rear end took up so much room, he was tightly wedged inside the sink and couldn't move at all.

He tried to get back onto the counter, but he was doubled up, and with his legs wriggling in the air, he could not push himself out. He knew it wouldn't do any good to call for help, because the waitress wouldn't come into the men's room. Besides, he would rather no one saw him, for although he couldn't see the bottoms of his feet, he was sure they must be very dirty. After much squirming, Wombat finally managed to push himself onto the counter, and he was quite out of breath by the time he scrambled quickly onto the wet floor.

He could find only paper towels to dry himself, which was all right for his hands and face, but he had to use the whole roll to dry the rest of his body. It seemed like a terrible waste of paper, and he thought a proper bath towel would be much better. He would have written

his suggestion to the management, if he had known how to spell "management," and he decided right then that he would learn how to spell the word, just as soon as he had the time.

Certain that he would be accepted now, he gathered up his clothes, and was about to leave the washroom when he heard a commotion in the lobby. Opening the door, he saw a man with a suitcase rushing past, and Wombat realized that the bus to the airport had arrived. Not wanting to waste any time, he hurried out of the bathroom and into the lobby without putting on his clothes. Outside the open door of the outpost,

Wombat could see the bus driver taking tickets from the people who were boarding the bus, and he looked around desperately for someone who might sell him a ticket.

He noticed a small room near the entrance of the building, where a man was sitting behind a desk. Thankful that he had found someone who would know about the ticket, Wombat ran toward him, but the bottoms of his feet were still wet, and he slipped on the wooden floor. He fell forward and slid up to the desk on all fours. In his fear of missing the bus, Wombat could only gasp as he stared up at the man, unable to make a sound. The man walked around the desk and looked down at Wombat, who appeared more matted than before with little pieces of paper towel clinging to his damp fur.

"How did you get in here?" the man shouted, waving his arms at Wombat. "Go on. Get out."

Wombat wanted to explain. He wanted to tell the man that he needed a ticket for the bus in a hurry. He wanted to tell him that he had to get to the airport because he did not want to wait any longer before seeing his family again.

But his voice did not come out in words, only in a series of squeaks.

"Go on. *Shoo!* Get out of here, you mangy wombat," cried the man, giving him a shove toward the door with his foot.

Wombat continued to slide on the floor as he hurried as quickly as he could to the outpost door. He thought that the driver might let him on the bus without a ticket, but as he was about to leave the building, he saw the door of the bus close. Then the bus pulled away.

"Wait," Wombat tried to shout, but his voice rose in a loud, unpleasant squeal.

He continued to squeak, as, running on all fours, he followed the bus for a short distance. Finally, he had to give up, and he scurried back into the bush. He stood up, and after brushing himself off, he put on his sweater.

He would not be able to go to the airport now, he realized. Not until his voice returned. *I'll just have to wait until I can say words that people understand again*, he told himself bravely. *But what if* – he thought suddenly. *What if my voice never gets better? What if I can never speak real words again?* Then, afraid he might never be able to go home, he began to squeal, while tears ran from his eyes into the fur on his cheeks.

Chapter 8

After Wombat traveled a couple of hours in the bush, he came upon a wombat tunnel. "We'll have to make do—" he squeaked, but then he stopped, remembering that Joey wasn't with him anymore. The bush felt different now that he was alone and no longer wished to join the wombats in the wild. He crawled into the empty tunnel and lay for a long time, unable to sleep. Finally, he started walking again, not sure where he was going. He thought it must be close to morning, although in the midst of the forest it was still very dark.

Suddenly, Wombat heard a loud, snarling scream a short distance behind him. He remembered hearing that sound once before, coming from the wide jaws of the Tasmanian devil. Terrified, he turned his head slowly to look behind. Sure enough, he could see the dark, moving outline of an animal between the trees. It was so close now that Wombat could hear the snapping of twigs and dry leaves beneath its feet.

Wombat found it difficult to run quickly, for the cold in his nose made it hard to breathe, and

the air in his open mouth cut his sore throat until he could not swallow. But just as he thought he was too tired to run any farther, the bush ended in farmland, and Wombat could see sheep grazing in the fields of grass. The first light of dawn shone on the roof of the farmhouse that stood on the far side of the pasture. And Wombat managed to run faster, knowing that help was nearby.

As he got closer to the farm, he could hear the sound of barking. *Dogs*, he thought with relief, for the Tasmanian devil had heard them too, and the creature had stopped to turn back at the edge of the woods. Wombat's legs ached, and he stumbled, falling on the wet, uneven ground. When he sat up, he found his sweater caked with yet another layer of mud.

Two dogs raced toward him, barking noisily. But when Wombat squeaked his greeting, their barks turned to growls, and Wombat recognized the unfriendly sounds that Sandalfoot always made at the neighbor's cat. Then the dogs' growls turned to snarls as they curled back their lips to show their teeth.

There was no place for Wombat to run, so he lay on the ground and curled into a ball. He lay very still, too frightened to move, and his chest became so tight that he was sure he had stopped breathing.

"Hey, you dogs! Be quiet there," a voice called out.

Wombat looked up as the dogs stopped their growling. He was thankful to see two people—a young boy in blue jeans carrying a leash and an older man in overalls carrying a gun. Wombat tried to stand to introduce himself, but he suddenly felt the barrel of the gun pressed against his back. Just then, he remembered his mother's warning at the airport gate: "Watch out for cars on the road and Tasmanian devils in the bush, and farmers with—" *And farmers with guns! That was the other* "*and,*" he realized, but now it was too late.

"Look at this, Joshua. Look what we've got here," the farmer said, nudging Wombat with his boot. "A filthy wombat. I guess there'll be one less wombat making holes in my fields tomorrow."

"Wait, Dad," the boy said. "This wombat's wearing a sweater. That's funny," he added with a laugh. "A wombat in a sweater? And look what else it's got." The boy gave the knapsack a poke with his finger, and then opened it. "Look at all this stuff. It even has a camera. Maybe the newspapers would pay us for a picture of the little fellow. Maybe they'd want one of us too, seeing as we're the ones who caught it."

The farmer scratched his head. "It could mean a little money for us."

"More than a little money, I bet," Joshua said excitedly. "Maybe enough for that new tractor you've been wanting. And maybe enough for a new bike and a camera too, like this one," added the boy, turning Wombat's camera over in his hands.

The farmer lowered his gun hesitantly. "But no one'll believe that we found a wombat in a

sweater and with its own knapsack too—not unless we show them. Better keep everything together, just as we found it." He thought for a moment. "All right, bring me a cage," he said finally. "But I'll shoot the wombat if it moves a hair."

While Wombat held his breath to keep his fur from moving, the boy hurried back to the farm. He returned soon with a cage, and then stepped toward Wombat. "Come on, you," he said. And to his surprise, Wombat crawled into the cage without a struggle. "Almost like it understands," Joshua said as he closed the door, after shoving Wombat's knapsack inside the cage.

"I *do*! I *do*!" Wombat squeaked, in a voice that sounded more like a sneeze than words. Then he coughed so hard that his eyes and nose began to run.

"Looks like we've got a sick animal on our hands," the man said. "We should probably wait a few days before telling the newspapers. A dead wombat in a sweater won't do us a bit of good." The man turned to his son. "This is your idea, so you'll be responsible for the creature." And after saying he would have to go tell his wife about the soon-to-be-famous wombat, the farmer carried the cage with Wombat into the barn. Then he hurried back to the farmhouse, and his son followed close behind to get Wombat some water.

Once he was alone, Wombat sat up and hugged his knapsack tightly to his chest. *The boy and his father don't seem to want to hurt me anymore*, he reassured himself. And they were also very understanding, for they must have known that Wombat wouldn't want his picture taken until his nose stopped running. *I will not try to speak again*, he decided, *until the reporters are here.* His voice should be normal by then, and he would be able to explain what had happened. *And once they've heard my story, they'll put me on a plane home*, he thought excitedly. *Probably with a wattle seed cookie because of the inconvenience they've caused me.*

Moments later, the boy came back with two bowls of water, a couple of rags, and a bar of soap. He took Wombat out of the cage and set him down in front of the smaller bowl. "There's water for you to drink," he said, and he watched while Wombat lapped up the water thirstily. Then he soaked one of the cloths in the other

water bowl, and after covering it with soap, he rubbed Wombat's fur with the wet cloth. Wombat did not mind being washed, even though the soap had a strong, unpleasant odor, without the slightest hint of apple blossoms that came from the soap Mary had given him.

"We need a tractor," Joshua said, as he dried Wombat's fur with the other cloth. "And I've never had a camera. But do you know what I would really like, if I had the money?" he added wistfully. "I'd like to go to a soccer camp, so I could learn to play better, and play in tournament games. Then I could travel with a team to different places and see a lot of things other than sheep."

It would be good for him to travel, Wombat thought sleepily as Joshua put him back inside the cage. *But someone should warn him about Tasmanian devils, and head colds, and cages.*

"But that's never going to happen," Joshua sighed. "I'll always have to stay here and help my father with the farm." He took the camera out of the knapsack and sat quietly looking at it again, until his father returned from the farmhouse.

"Your mother told me not to bother with the newspapers," the farmer said. "She said to phone the zoo instead."

"The zoo? But what if they won't give us any money? Did you ask them about the money?" Joshua asked, becoming upset.

"Yes, there'll be some money," his father replied. "And after they've seen the camera, you'll be getting it as a reward. That's if you can get the animal well again."

"But if the newspapers don't come, no one's going to believe that I found a wombat in a sweater," Joshua said sadly.

"Give me the camera," his father said, taking it from his son's hands. "I'll take your picture so you'll have the proof when we get the camera back."

Joshua smiled and sat as close to the cage as he could. Wombat felt too sick to sit up, but he tried to smile too, for he wanted to look his best.

"Which zoo is he going to?" the boy asked, after his father had snapped the picture.

"The one in Melbourne wants the wombat just as soon as it's well," the man replied, putting the camera back into Wombat's knapsack.

Wombat almost cried out in his excitement. What luck! In a few days, he would be back on the mainland of Australia. Once he was there, he would be able to get a plane home.

"The mainland? That's too far away," the boy mumbled, for he wanted to be able to visit Wombat sometimes.

"The wombat will be a lot farther away than Melbourne. It's only going to be there a week or two," his father said. "There's a zoo in China that's been wanting a wombat. They're willing to trade a panda for this strange little fellow."

China! Wombat stared out at Joshua and his father, too startled to speak even if he *could* have spoken. He didn't know anything about China, except that it was far away. If he had known this was going to happen, he would have learned to speak Chinese. He made up his mind right then, that when he got away, he would learn to speak Chinese, just as soon as he had the time. *If I get away*, he reminded himself sadly, for he was beginning to wonder if he would ever see his family again.

Chapter 9

The next day, Wombat felt much worse. Sometimes he felt too hot, and then sometimes he felt like he would never get warm again. His nose, which had become warm and rough, continued to run. And because Joshua had not thought to bring Wombat a box of tissues, Wombat had to wipe his nose on the sleeve of his sweater when no one was looking, for he did not want Joshua to think that he would have done that at home. As Wombat grew sicker, his sweater became dirtier and damper, and he was thankful when Joshua arrived with some new clothing.

"I brought you something dry to wear," Joshua said, as he pulled the sweater off over Wombat's head. "This is mine," he said, holding out a shirt. Without getting up, Wombat tried to raise his arm. But instead of helping Wombat put on the shirt, the boy placed it over him like a cover.

"And you haven't been eating your leaves. I guess you aren't strong enough to chew," Joshua said. "So I brought you something else," he said, as he held up the steaming mug that he had brought into the barn. "Mother says this should help make you strong again." He drew a small amount of liquid into a child's medicine syringe, and as Wombat lay on his side, the boy placed the tip of the syringe onto Wombat's tongue. Wombat shivered as an unexpected bitter taste filled his mouth.

"It's a wattle seed drink," Joshua said. "You need it to get your strength back."

Wattle seed? It didn't taste like the cookies the lady on the plane had given him, but once Wombat knew what the liquid was, he was able to drink the whole mug from the syringe.

* * *

The boy patiently fed Wombat five times a day for three more days, before Wombat began to get better and feel like his normal self. His sniffles were gone, and his throat no longer itched. And best of all, he had enough energy to eat the leaves and grass the boy brought him.

"The wombat's well enough to go now," the farmer said one morning when he went to the barn, where his son was sitting beside the cage.

"Can't he stay a little longer?" Joshua asked hopefully. "He needs more looking after."

"No. It's time for him to go," his father said gently. "I've phoned the zoo, and someone is going to meet me at the airport in a few hours."

"Let me go with you," Joshua begged.

"No. You've done well enough, and now you have other work to do here," his father replied. Before his son could argue, the farmer left to move the truck closer to the barn door.

The boy put Wombat's sweater into the knapsack. "I'll miss you. I wish you didn't have to go," he said hoarsely. "But I'll try to go to China someday and visit you at the zoo," he promised quickly as the truck arrived outside the door of the barn. "You can keep the shirt," he added, pulling it around Wombat to make sure he was completely covered. "It's my most comfortable one, but you'll need it more than I will." Then Joshua carried Wombat's cage out of the barn, and the farmer lifted it onto the back of the open truck. And as they drove away, Wombat could hear Joshua calling good-bye.

***

The man from the zoo was already waiting when they arrived at the airport. He stared curiously into the cage at Wombat, who was still lying down, for the ride in the back of the truck had made him feel a little dizzy. "Looks just like an ordinary wombat to me," the man from the zoo said.

"How many wombats have you seen with a backpack?" the farmer asked. He opened the door of the cage and took out the knapsack. "And this is what he was wearing when I found him," he added, pulling out Wombat's sweater.

Wombat became upset as he watched the men look through all of his things, but when

they touched his sweater, his camera, and his bar of apple blossom soap, he wanted to shout at them to stop. *Those are my special things. Those were presents from my family—from my mother, and my father, and my sister, Mary.* He did not try to say anything, however, for he had to save his voice until he reached the zoo in Melbourne.

"Come into the airport while we fill out the papers," the man from the zoo said as he closed the latch at the top of the cage.

"Shouldn't you be putting the padlock on?" the farmer asked. "I'll not be getting the money if the wombat gets out."

"We won't be long," the man from the zoo replied. Then he laughed. "Besides, it's just an animal. It's not smart like you and me." Leaving Wombat's knapsack on the truck beside the cage, the two men turned and walked away.

For a moment after the men had disappeared from his sight, Wombat stood, not knowing what to do. Then, with a loud cry, he flung himself against the bars of the cage. He turned and charged backward toward the door, hitting it with all his strength. He slammed his rear end against the door again and again, but it would not open. Then, he stopped.

Why am I doing this, he wondered? *Why am I trying to break down the door when all I have to do is lift up the latch?*

Wombat reached out and slipped his arm

between the bars of his cage, but he could not find what he was looking for. Then he heard the men returning. Desperately, he stretched his arm up, trying to reach farther, trying to stay calm even though the men were almost at the truck. Finally, he felt the latch beneath his hand. He pushed it up, and the door swung open.

He decided to wear the shirt the boy had given him, and he stuffed the dirty sweater into the knapsack. *Oh, no. The front's on the back and the back's on the front*, Wombat realized with embarrassment when he looked down and found that in his hurry to dress he had put the shirt on the wrong way around. There was no time to change it, and he quickly put on his hat and climbed down from the back of the truck. Keeping his face turned away, he hurried into the airport past the men, who were engrossed in a conversation and did not notice him.

As soon as he entered the airport, he rushed into the washroom, and taking off his shirt, he turned it so the front was at the front where it was supposed to be. This time, because the boy had bathed him, Wombat's hands and face were clean, and with his shirt turned the right way around, he was properly dressed for travel. He cleared his throat, wondering if he could speak, for although his cold was better, his voice had not been used for a long time. He went up to the man at the ticket counter, and, clearing his throat again, very carefully formed a word: "Please."

Delighted to hear the word leave his mouth without a single squeak, Wombat repeated himself. "Please, sir," he said. "I would like a ticket to the mainland."

He did not have to wait long before boarding

the plane that would take him back to Melbourne. The plane lifted into the air, and as Wombat Smith watched comfortably from his seat by the window, the two men searched for a knapsack-carrying wombat that had disappeared.

Chapter 10

Wombat didn't have any trouble getting a plane from Australia to the city he called home, for he followed the instructions his mother had given him. He had a seat by the window again, but Wombat was disappointed to learn that the person who had the seat beside him did not have any wattle seed cookies. The trip home seemed to get longer the more impatient he became, but at last the plane arrived at the airport.

He was thankful to get a taxi from the airport right away, and it wasn't long before the driver stopped in front of Wombat's house. After paying the money he owed for the fare, Wombat got out of the taxi and hurried up the walkway. He was glad he had decided not to wear the red sweater his mother had given him, for he would have been embarrassed if she had seen it looking so dirty. He walked up the steps, and he was about to open the front door, when suddenly, becoming more excited, he felt a strange, nervous feeling in his stomach.

What if no one recognizes me, he thought, remembering his own shock at the outpost when he saw himself in the bathroom mirror. *What if they do not want me back?* Too afraid to go in, he ran back down the walkway.

Then he heard a dog barking. It was an angry sound, like the bark of the dogs that had chased him across the farmer's field. Wombat ran, but as he raced across the front lawn and onto the sidewalk, the dog continued to chase him. Wombat's legs would not move any faster, and finally, the dog caught up. He felt the dog's front paws hitting against his back, and Wombat was knocked to the ground.

Wombat lay very still with his eyes closed as the dog sniffed the farm smells on Joshua's shirt. Then he could feel his hat being sniffed, and then the fur on the side of his face. He closed his eyes more tightly, expecting to feel the dog's sharp teeth on his ears. Instead, he heard a whimper and felt a wet tongue licking his cheeks and nose. Wombat opened one eye a small amount and saw a familiar eye looking back at him. Then, opening both eyes very wide, he recognized the nose that was pressed close to his face.

"Sandalfoot," he cried, sitting up.

"Sandalfoot," he heard a girl call as she ran toward them. "I'm sorry," she called to Wombat. "He won't hurt you. Sandalfoot, come here."

When the girl reached them, Wombat realized who she was. "Mary," he cried excitedly.

The girl stopped, and for a moment she stared at him without speaking. "Wombat!" she exclaimed in surprise. Then she knelt beside him, and laughing delightedly, wrapped her arms around him. Finally, she lifted him to his feet, and as Sandalfoot danced noisily around them, she pulled Wombat down the street to their house.

His mother was surprised too, when she saw him standing in the hall, and she rushed to pull him close to her. She had just finished giving Wombat a kiss on the nose when Mr. Smith walked through the front door. There was a sudden loud thump as Mr. Smith's briefcase hit the floor.

In a moment, Wombat's father was over the shock of finding Wombat there. "I'm glad you are safely home with us," he said, giving Wombat a big hug.

"I hope you didn't have any trouble in the bush," Mrs. Smith said in a worried voice.

"Did you see any wombats when you were there?" Mary asked.

"I'll tell you everything after I've had a bath with the soap you gave me," Wombat replied.

Wombat went into his bedroom and saw that it was just the same as he had left it. After taking off his hat and Joshua's shirt, he laid them on the chair by his bed and went into the bathroom. While he washed his sweater in the sink, his sister ran a bath of warm water with sweet-smelling bubbles. Then Wombat sank down into the tub and watched the bubbles turn brown as the dirt slid from his fur. After he'd finished scrubbing himself all over, even the fur between his toes, he dried himself with a big, fluffy bath towel, put on a fresh set of clothing, and ran down the stairs to have his dinner.

"Did you have a nice bath, dear?" Mrs. Smith asked as Wombat climbed onto the thick pillow that was still on his chair at the dining room table.

"Yes. It's nice that the tub is big enough to sit in," he replied.

After tucking the napkin under his chin, he leaned close enough to his bowl of salad to smell the garlic dressing. "Did you know that wombats never put dressing on their salads?" he asked as he took the first bite. "Or eat with forks at dining room tables?" He closed his eyes as the taste of the garlic filled his mouth. "I may look like a wombat on the outside," he said finally, "but I look more like a Smith on the inside."

Then Wombat began to tell them about his stay in the bush with the wombats and Joey. But when he told them about his escape from the Tasmanian devil, his mother interrupted him.

"We were so worried," she said. "We were

afraid we might never see you again."

"You wouldn't have—unless I'd learned to speak Chinese," Wombat replied, and because his family looked confused, he added quickly, "but only if I'd traded places with the panda." Then he told them how frightened he had been when he heard he was going to be sent to the zoo in China. "It's not that I didn't want to see China, or meet the panda," he explained. "And I would like to go to China someday—but not inside a cage."

"I'd like to meet the panda too," Mary said, jumping down from her chair and running to her father. "Please, can't we go to China and see the panda?"

"Well, perhaps a trip to China would be a good idea," Mr. Smith said thoughtfully.

"Yes," Mrs. Smith agreed. "But we will have to wait until Wombat is well rested before he starts out on another adventure."

Then Wombat remembered that Joshua had mentioned going to China too. *Maybe I will see him there*, he thought excitedly. *Of course, Joshua only wanted to go to China to see me in the zoo*, Wombat remembered. *But maybe he won't mind too much if we see the panda instead.*

Then Wombat told them about being sick and losing his voice. And about the boy who had saved his life and had given Wombat his best shirt to wear.

"We should do something to thank him," Mrs. Smith said. "Can you think of something that the boy might like?"

"He would like a camera," Wombat replied, remembering the reward that Joshua was supposed to get. "And a bicycle," he added. "And a tractor for the farm."

"Are you sure there isn't anything else he wants?" Wombat's father asked with a laugh.

"He wants to go to a soccer camp," Wombat replied. "That's what he wants more than anything else."

Mr. Smith thought for a moment. "Well, then maybe there is something I can do for him," he said. "Your mother and I have a friend in Tasmania who coaches a soccer team. I am sure he will get in touch with your new friend, if you give me the boy's name."

"Joshua," Wombat said happily. Then he

paused, realizing that he did not know Joshua's last name or address.

"There is nothing I can do unless I have his last name," Mr. Smith said. "I'm sorry, but we won't be able to find Joshua without it."

Mary ran to Wombat and handed him a chocolate cookie. "I'm glad the boy made you all better," she whispered, trying to cheer him up. Then she put her arms around him. "And I'm glad you came home again."

"I'm glad I went," Wombat said, "but I'm gladder to be home where I belong."

✷✷✷

Later that night, as Wombat picked up Joshua's shirt from the chair, he noticed there was something in the pocket. He felt inside the shirt and discovered a small envelope about the size of a gift card or an invitation. It was empty, but on the front was written the boy's name, Joshua Shepard, and the address of the farm.

My father will be able to get Joshua on the soccer team after all, he thought happily as he crawled into bed.

He could not wait to tell Joshua the good news, and he decided to write him a letter the next day. And maybe Joshua would write him back, he thought contentedly as he began to drift into sleep. Now Joshua would always be his friend.

Then he sat up, wide awake again. He had never told Joshua that his last name was Smith. How was Joshua to know who had sent the letter? *And what if Joshua doesn't remember me? What if Joshua never writes back?*

He lay back down sadly, wondering what he might do. Then suddenly, he remembered the photo that the farmer had taken of him with Joshua. He would send Joshua a copy and sign it too. "To Joshua: Thank you for looking after me when I was sick. Wombat Smith." Then Joshua would be sure to remember him.

And he would have a copy of the picture for himself, although he probably wouldn't sign it. *It would look very nice in a picture frame*, he thought. If he had a picture frame. And he decided right then that he would get a frame for the picture, just as soon as he had the time.

The End